NIGHT TRAIN

NIGHT TRAIN

STORY BY CAROLINE STUTSON

ILLUSTRATIONS BY KATHERINE TILLOTSON

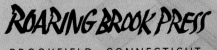

ROARING BROOK PRESS

BROOKFIELD, CONNECTICUT

Thunder
Lightning
On the tracks...

Here comes the train!
Watch out. Stand back.

Step up.
Step up before it leaves.

All aboard!

Tickets, please.

With jumps and bumps
We start our ride,
Speeding through
The countryside.

Grassy meadows
Horses
Barns...
Cows and sheep
In their backyards.

Bridges
Tunnels

Station stops.

Window towns
With rows of shops.

Cars and trucks that watch us rush,
Wishing they
Could speed like us.

To the diner...

Have a seat.
Order what you'd like to eat.

Covered dishes.
Plates stacked high.

Dining while the miles fly by.

Back we go
On rattling floors.

Car

To car
Through hissing doors.

In the bathroom,
Silver sinks.

Taking
Shaking paper drinks.

Dozing
Waking
Through the night.

Dozing
Waking...

Station lights!

Hurry! Hurry!
Step with care.

Sad
And happy.
Safely there.

Bright skyscrapers.
City dawn.

There it goes.
Our train moves on...

For my mother, Randy, with love and thanks for intoducing me to trains

—C.S.

With all my love to Bob

—K.T.

A NEAL PORTER BOOK

Text copyright © 2002 by Caroline Stutson
Illustrations copyright © 2002 by Katherine Tillotson

Published by Roaring Brook Press
A Division of The Millbrook Press, 2 Old New Milford Road, Brookfield, Connecticut 06804

Library of Congress Cataloging-in-Publication Data
Stutson, Caroline.
Night Train / story by Caroline Stutson; illustrations by Katherine Tillotson.
p.   cm.
Summary; Rhyming text presents a nighttime train ride through the countryside, with lightning
on the tracks, rattling cars, and the welcoming lights of the station at the end of the journey.
[1. Railroads—Fiction.   2. Stories in rhyme.]   I. Tillotson, Katherine, ill.   II. Title.
PZ8.3.S925   Ni 2002   [E]—dc21   2001048295

Designed by Jennifer Browne
Printed in Hong Kong

ISBN 0-7613-1598-5 (trade)
10 9 8 7 6 5 4 3 2 1

ISBN 0-7613-2662-6 (library binding)
10 9 8 7 6 5 4 3 2 1

First edition